Mrs Pepperpot and the Ma

A Beaver Book
Published by Arrow Books Limited
62-65 Chandos Place, London WC2N 4NW

An imprint of Century Hutchinson Ltd

London Melbourne Sydney Auckland Johannesburg
and agencies throughout the world

This edition first published in 1987
by Hutchinson Children's Books
Beaver edition 1989

Set in 14/17pt Palatino

Made and printed in Great Britain
by Scotprint, Musselburgh, Scotland

ISBN 0 09 959770 5

Mrs Pepperpot and the Macaroni

Alf Prøysen

Illustrated by David Arthur

BEAVER BOOKS

'It's a very long time since we've had macaroni for supper,' said Mr Pepperpot one day.

'Then you shall have it today, my love,' said his wife. 'But I shall have to go to the grocer for some. So first of all you'll have to find me.'

'Find you?' said Mr Pepperpot. 'What sort of nonsense is that?' But when he looked round for her he couldn't see her anywhere.

'Don't be silly, Wife,' he said; 'if you're hiding in
the cupboard you must come out this minute.
We're too big to play hide-and-seek.'

'*I'm* not too big, I'm just the right size for "hunt-
the-pepperpot",' laughed Mrs Pepperpot. 'Find me
if you can!'

'I'm not going to charge round my own bedroom
looking for my wife,' he said crossly.

'Now, now! I'll help you; I'll tell you when you're
warm. Just now you're very cold.' For Mr
Pepperpot was peering out of the window,
thinking she might have jumped out. As he
searched round the room she called out, 'Warm!
Colder! Getting hotter!' until he was quite dizzy.

At last she shouted, 'You'll burn the top of your bald head if you don't look up!' And there she was, sitting on the bedpost, swinging her legs and laughing at him.

Her husband pulled a very long face when he saw her. 'This is a bad business – a very bad business,' he said, stroking her cheek with his little finger.

'I don't think it's a bad business,' said Mrs Pepperpot.

'I shall have a terrible time. The whole town will laugh when they see I have a wife the size of a pepperpot.'

'Who cares?' she answered. 'That doesn't matter a bit. Now put me down on the floor so that I can get ready to go to the grocer and buy your macaroni.'

But her husband wouldn't hear of her going; he would go to the grocer himself.

'That'll be a lot of use!' she said. 'When you get home you'll have forgotten to buy the macaroni. I'm sure even if I wrote "macaroni" right across your forehead you'd bring back cinnamon and salt herrings instead.'

'But how are you going to walk all that way with those tiny legs?'

'Put me in your coat pocket; then I won't need to walk.'

There was no help for it, so Mr Pepperpot put his wife in his pocket and set off for the shop.

Soon she started talking: 'My goodness me, what a lot of strange things you have in your pocket – screws and nails, tobacco and matches – there's even a fish-hook! You'll have to take that out at once; I might get it caught in my skirt.'

'Don't talk so loud,' said her husband as he took out the fish-hook. 'We're going into the shop now.'

It was an old-fashioned village store where they sold everything from prunes to coffee cups. The grocer was particularly proud of the coffee cups and held one up for Mr Pepperpot to see.

This made his wife curious and she popped her head out of his pocket.

'You stay where you are!' whispered Mr Pepperpot.

'I beg your pardon, did you say anything?' asked the grocer.

'No, no, I was just humming a little tune,' said Mr Pepperpot. 'Tra-la-la!'

'What colour are the cups?' whispered his wife. And her husband sang:

'The cups are blue
With gold edge too,
But they cost too much
So that won't do!'

After that Mrs Pepperpot kept quiet – but not for long. When her husband pulled out his tobacco tin she couldn't resist hanging on to the lid. Neither her husband nor anyone else in the shop noticed her slipping on to the counter and hiding behind a flour bag. From there she darted silently across to the scales, crawled under them, past a pair of kippers wrapped in newspaper, and found herself next to the coffee cups.

'Aren't they pretty!' she whispered, and took a step backwards to get a better view. Whoops! She fell right into the macaroni drawer which had been left open. She hastily covered herself up with macaroni, but the grocer heard the scratching noise and quickly banged the drawer shut.

You see, it did sometimes happen that mice got in the drawers, and that's not the sort of thing you want people to know about, so the grocer pretended nothing had happened and went on serving.

There was Mrs Pepperpot all in the dark; she could hear the grocer serving her husband now. That's good, she thought. When he orders macaroni I'll get my chance to slip into the bag with it.

But it was just as she had feared; her husband forgot what he had come to buy. Mrs Pepperpot shouted at the top of her voice, 'MACARONI!' but it was impossible to get him to hear.

'A quarter of a pound of coffee, please,' said her husband.

'Anything else?' asked the grocer.

'MACARONI!' shouted Mrs Pepperpot.

'Two pounds of sugar,' said her husband.

'Anything more?'

'MACARONI!' shouted Mrs Pepperpot.

But at last her husband remembered the macaroni of his own accord. The grocer hurriedly filled a bag. He thought he felt something move, but he didn't say a word.

'That's all, thank you,' said Mr Pepperpot. When he got outside the door he was just about to make sure his wife was still in his pocket when a van drew up and offered to give him a lift all the way home.

Once there he took off his knapsack with all the shopping in it and put his hand in his pocket to lift out his wife.

The pocket was empty.

Now he was really frightened. First he thought she was teasing him, but when he had called three times and still no wife appeared, he put on his hat again and hurried back to the shop.

The grocer saw him coming. He's probably going to complain about the mouse in the macaroni, he thought.

'Have you forgotten anything, Mr Pepperpot?' he asked, and smiled as pleasantly as he could.

Mr Pepperpot was looking all round. 'Yes,' he said.

'I would be very grateful, Mr Pepperpot, if you would keep it to yourself about the mouse being in the macaroni. I'll let you have these fine blue coffee cups if you'll say no more about it.'

'Mouse?' Mr Pepperpot looked puzzled.

'Shh!' said the grocer, and hurriedly started wrapping up the cups.

Then Mr Pepperpot realized that the grocer had mistaken his wife for a mouse. So he took the cups and rushed home as fast as he could. By the time he got there he was in a sweat of fear that his wife might have been squeezed to death in the macaroni bag.

'Oh, my dear wife,' he muttered to himself. 'My poor darling wife. I'll never again be ashamed of you being the size of a pepperpot – as long as you're still alive!'

When he opened the door she was standing by the cooking-stove, dishing up the macaroni – as large as life; in fact, as large as you or I.

Other titles in the Beaver/Sparrow Picture Book series: